Crazy About German Shepherds

Crazy About German Shepherds

Brent Ashabranner

Photographs by

Jennifer Ashabranner

Cobblehill Books

Dutton • New York

Library of Congress Cataloging-in-Publication Data
Ashabranner, Brent K., date
Crazy about German Shepherds / Brent Ashabranner ; photographs by
Jennifer Ashabranner.
p.   cm.
Summary: A girl describes her experiences opening her own kennel
in the Blue Ridge Mountains to raise German Shepherds.
ISBN 0-525-65032-6
1. German shepherd dogs—Juvenile literature.
[1. German shepherd dogs.   2. Dogs—Breeding.]
I. Ashabranner, Jennifer, ill.   II. Title.
SF429.G37A74   1990
636.7'37—dc20   90-1303
CIP   AC

Published in the United States by
Cobblehill Books, an affiliate of Dutton Children's Books,
a division of Penguin Books USA Inc.
Published simultaneously in Canada by
Fitzhenry & Whiteside Limited, Toronto
Designed by Joy Taylor
Printed in the United States of America   First Edition
10   9   8   7   6   5   4   3   2   1

Contents

One	Peggy's Place	3
Two	Getting Started	17
Three	Zoe	26
Four	A Note on Names	35
Five	Mountain Full of Puppies	40
Six	Letting Them Go	55
Seven	Training	59
Eight	Having Fun	66
Nine	Zoe Saves the Day	73
Ten	A Letter from Peggy	81
	Bibliography	83
	Index	85

For Muriel O'Callaghan

Crazy About German Shepherds

Dare in the classic German shepherd pose.

One

Peggy's Place

Jennifer and I drove up the mountain to Peggy's place one golden morning in April. The dirt road was terrible in patches, but Jennifer's little Mercury Tracer took the bumps and the curves confidently; and since Jennifer was driving, I could enjoy this lovely foothill country of the northern Virginia Blue Ridge Mountains. Dogwood and redbud were in bloom. Along the roadside were violets, wild geranium, and the pink blossoms of trailing arbutus. Tall, white, wild flowers and fragile-looking blue ones, neither of which I could identify, grew close to the road.

We went down a steep hill, around a sharp curve, and were at Peggy's. The road into her place is barred by a sturdy wooden gate. As Jennifer drove up to it and stopped, four German shepherds bounded from different parts of the yard, greeting us noisily. There was no need for Jennifer to honk.

Peggy heard the commotion and came from a kennel and fenced run area I could see at the back of her property. She ordered the dogs away from the gate, made them sit on a grassy bank beside the driveway, then opened the gate for us. Jennifer drove to the house, the dogs charging along behind us.

When we got out of the car, the German shepherds greeted Jennifer like the old friend that she is, then turned their curiosity toward me, a stranger to them. Peggy told the dogs firmly, but without raising her voice, to be good, and I stood quietly while they sniffed until they were satisfied. After that we sat on the porch of Peggy's house, and each dog was introduced to me formally: Dare, Zoe, Coyote, Freesia. Zoe is a Greek name pronounced Zo-e, and Freesia is pronounced Free-zuh, like the flower she was named for.

Peggy told me a little about each dog. "Dare is the oldest and the dominant dog. None of the others can shove her around without being put in their place very quickly. Once when Zoe was pestering Dare down at the pond, Dare just took her paw and pushed Zoe's head under the water. Zoe is Dare's daughter; she's a sweetheart, very affectionate. She loves to be touched and to touch you. Whenever Jennifer spends the night here, Zoe shares the couch with her.

"Coyote is Dare's son, but he is younger than Zoe, from a later litter. Being the only male with three females doesn't seem to bother him. He's very self-confident, but he's not a fighter. He's a big marshmallow really. Freesia is Zoe's daughter. She's the youngest of the four, but not much younger than Coyote. She's agile and fast and plays rough. She likes the company of the other dogs, and she considers Coyote her personal property."

The dogs listened intently as Peggy talked about them.

Zoe. *Coyote.*

Each time a name was mentioned, the one being described seemed to lean forward and study Peggy's face, as if trying to fathom what she was saying. With such beautiful, intelligent-looking animals, it was easy to imagine that they understood very well.

Since this was my first visit to Peggy's place, she showed me around. We walked first to the kennels with their fenced runs behind her house, the four dogs trooping along with us. There are four kennels and runs in which she puts her dogs when there is need to confine them and which she uses when she is taking care of a dog for a friend or a grooming customer.

A quiet moment with Freesia.

"I just 'dog sit,' " Peggy explained. "I don't ever intend to become a boarding kennel. That's no fun, too much trouble, too much hassle."

While we were talking, Peggy put the finishing touches on a new kennel that she had been building when we arrived. She had Dare go into the kennel and then crawled in after her to show us how much room there was, even for a big dog. Dare at first seemed puzzled by Peggy's strange behavior, then placidly accepted it.

Peggy showed me her garden, where in the right season she grows beans, tomatoes, cucumbers, peppers, asparagus, and other vegetables. In the upper part of her yard, she has started a small orchard, and sometimes Jennifer brings her a new tree to plant.

Dare inspects a new kennel (inset) and Peggy and Dare demonstrate how roomy it is.

Jennifer's Kumar in friendly confrontation with a sheep belonging to one of Peggy's neighbors.

Once Jennifer had a little Lhasa Apso named Kumar who became great pals with one of Peggy's first German shepherds, a big female named Bones. On weekends when Jennifer came up, Kumar and Bones had wonderful good times playing together, exploring game trails on Peggy's ten-acre property, swimming in the pond below her house. The Odd Couple, Jennifer and Peggy called them. Now Kumar is buried beneath a plum tree in Peggy's orchard. Bones is buried nearby beneath a Granny Smith apple tree.

In the house, Peggy showed me the whelping room, which is a big walk-in closet in her bedroom. Dare and Zoe have had all their litters there, and Freesia will soon occupy it with her first litter. Zoe, Freesia, and Coyote were born there. The dogs had followed us into the house, and they were as interested in the whelping room as I was. After all, it is a very special room for them.

I asked Peggy if the dogs had the run of the house. "There are rules, and they know them," Peggy said, "but, yes, I do let them stay in the house. They are pets and companions, and they wouldn't be nearly as much fun or company for me if I kept them outside all the time. Each one of them knows how to open the door, both to come in and go out, so letting them in and out is not a bother for me."

After inspecting the whelping closet, we went to the grooming room where five days a week, Tuesday through Saturday, Peggy clips, combs, washes, and generally makes all breeds of dogs beautiful and clean. The grooming room is a big converted utility room at the front end of the house, and it is filled with a grooming table, tubs, kennels, and tools. Peggy picks dogs up from the town of Front Royal and other places, grooms them, and delivers them back to their owners. Grooming is the principal source of her income, though some money comes in from obedience training and dog sitting.

Peggy grooms cats as well as dogs. She has never lost the liking for cats that she had as a girl.

"If I make any profit selling puppies, that is just luck," Peggy said. "Raising German shepherds is a labor of love, not a business."

This was Monday, and Peggy had no dogs to groom, so we ate a leisurely lunch. I already knew a good deal about Peggy, but now she filled in the details for me. She grew up in Alexandria, Virginia, the Washington, D.C., suburb where Jennifer now lives. "We never had a German shepherd when I was a girl," Peggy said, "but we did have a great beagle named Kim. My brothers and sisters and I taught him all kinds of tricks. His reward was Oreo cookies, and he couldn't resist them. But I was really a cat person in those days. I drove my parents crazy dragging home every stray cat I found on the street."

After she graduated from high school, Peggy wasn't sure what she wanted to do. She drifted into Vietnam War protest activity, helping raise money for publishing anti-war newspapers. The death of one of her brothers in Vietnam plunged her into personal despair and reinforced her commitment to war protest. In time, she moved to Charlottesville, Virginia, where she worked in an office to make enough money to live on while she continued her war protest activity on the side.

It was in Charlottesville that the first German shepherd came into Peggy's life. When she arrived home from work one afternoon—she was living in a house outside the city because the rent was cheap—a big dog, a male German shepherd, was sitting in the yard. She had never seen him before and assumed that he belonged to one of the families in this semirural area. As she went into the house, she said, "Hi, fella," and he responded with a thump of his tail.

When Peggy came out two hours later, the German shepherd was still there. Later that night she looked out and saw him lying near the porch. She found some leftover stew in the frig and offered it to him. He ate hungrily and thumped his tail. Peggy decided that he must be lost or abandoned, though she could not imagine anyone abandoning such a beautiful dog.

"If you're going to stay around, I have to call you something," she said. Since he was far too big and dignified to be called Doggie, she called him Doran (pronounced Dorn) because he reminded her of a friend with that name who sometimes dropped in on her unannounced—as the dog had done.

Doran stayed, and Peggy found that the big German shepherd was a wonderful companion. She hoped she could keep him, but she knew he would never really belong to her unless she tried to find his owner. She inquired at the animal shelter and the police and even advertised in the newspaper, describing Doran and giving her phone number. The police and animal shelter had no missing dog report that fitted Doran, and no one called about her ad.

After a week, Peggy began to believe that Doran was hers, and then one day a Federal Express driver delivered a package to her house. He saw Doran and asked about him. Peggy told him how she came to have him, and the man said he thought he knew the owner. As it turned out, he did. A woman who lived twenty miles away had lost her German shepherd. She had papers and pictures, and Doran clearly knew her.

He went with his owner, but Peggy never forgot him. "That was a bad time," she said. "I missed Doran. I didn't like my job. The war protest took an emotional toll. I had a romance with a guy that went nowhere, and that took a bigger toll. I was stressed out. I got sick, and my doctor said I was on the verge of ulcers. He told me in no uncertain terms that I had to change my style of life."

What Peggy did was move to another town in Virginia— Manassas, which is near Bull Run, the site of two Civil War battles. In Manassas she began working as a house painter with some friends who had started a successful house-painting business. "Believe me," Peggy said, "that was a change of life-style. It was probably also the beginning of a feeling that I would rather work for myself—like I'm doing here on the mountain—than for someone else."

As soon as she had saved enough money, Peggy bought a German shepherd puppy and named him Doran. She trained him, using a book on obedience training that she got from the library. "That was a traumatic experience for both of us," Peggy said, "but it taught me that I was really interested in dogs and that the German shepherd was my kind of dog."

When he was six months old, Doran was hit by a car, an

accident that shattered one of his hind legs. A veterinary surgeon tried to repair the leg, but it never again functioned properly, even though Peggy invested in more costly surgery. "I felt terrible," Peggy said, "but the experience made me want to learn more about veterinarians and what they do."

She quit house painting and went to work as a veterinarian's assistant in Manassas. She worked for the veterinarian three years, scrubbing the hospital every day, feeding the dogs, assisting in surgery, learning about medicines, beginning to learn some of the elements of grooming.

She began working weekends at the kennel near Manassas where she had bought Doran. She cleaned the kennels, fed the dogs, and did all the bathing and grooming. Now she was working seven days a week with dogs and learning more all the time about German shepherds. Occasionally the kennel owners would ask Peggy to take a potential show puppy home on weekends to help in its human socialization, important to prepare it for the long hours it would eventually spend in the judging ring at dog shows.

She still had Doran, but while Peggy was working at the kennel she bought another German shepherd puppy, a female that she named Bones. When I asked Peggy about the unusual name, she laughed and said, "It would take too long to explain. I named her for a friend who used to gamble a lot."

"Gamble," I said. "Dice. Bones."

Peggy laughed again. "Yes," she said, but didn't go into any more detail.

Peggy had developed a strong interest in training as a result of having trained Doran with only a book as a guide. The nearby Northern Virginia Community College offered a course in dog obedience training, and Peggy signed up with Bones. Bones graduated top dog in the class. Bones had also

Family portrait.

produced a litter of puppies while Peggy was living and working in Manassas. It was at about this time that Peggy began to think about having a place of her own, a rural place, where she could raise German shepherds, have a grooming business, and perhaps do obedience training.

Now we had finished lunch and were back outside. Dare was standing beside Peggy. Zoe had found something interesting to sniff at behind the kennels. Freesia was teasing Coyote up near the gate, but he did not seem to mind very much. I looked around at the house, the kennels, the garden and young orchard, the woods that hid the pond on the lower part of her property.

"And this is the result of the dream," I said. "I think I can call it a dream."

"This is the result," Peggy said, "and, yes, you can call it a dream."

JENNIFER and I had talked for a long time about telling Peggy's story in words and photographs. Driving down the mountain that afternoon, I said to Jennifer, "Let's do it. You take the pictures; I'll write the words, but they are going to be Peggy's words."

And they are. The voice you will hear in the pages ahead is Peggy's.

Two

Getting Started

I KNEW what I wanted: a rural place with enough room to raise German shepherds, a place close enough to affluent urban centers for me to build a grooming business, teach classes in obedience training, and, in time, raise and sell puppies. The place I found had all those things. Perched up on the mountain, it is as rural as anyone could want, but is is only a little over an hour's drive from the well-to-do Virginia suburbs of Washington, D.C. It is just a few miles from the growing town of Front Royal, the gateway to Shenandoah National Park. It is near the wealthy northern Virginia hunt country; Middleburg—a lovely town of smart shops and a fine eighteenth-century inn—is the unofficial capital of hunt country and less than an hour away.

The place was in a setting of natural beauty and had all kinds of potential for more beauty. The whole mountain had

Bones and Kumar having fun on a summer day.

been carved up into ten-acre tracts, so everyone had elbow room. Some of the residents of the mountain had apple and peach orchards; some had vineyards and fields of blueberries and strawberries. Some were professional people from Washington who just had weekend cabins. Besides a nice pond, the place I wanted has three springs on it and a year-round stream. The whole mountain is crisscrossed by game trails and old wagon trails. The Appalachian Trail, the famous two-thousand-mile-long hikers' trail that stretches from Maine to Georgia, runs right by the place I already thought of as mine. The house on the place would need some changes for my purposes, but that could be taken care of.

There were just two problems. One was that I didn't have enough money to buy the place. The other was that it wasn't for sale even if I had had the money. But it was for rent—I had learned about it from a rent ad in the newspaper—and the rent was reasonable, an amount I could afford. One summer day, Bones, Doran, and I moved in as renters.

I took a job at a good, busy grooming shop in Vienna, a Virginia suburb of Washington, D.C. I had to drive a hundred miles round-trip five days a week, but that was a small price to pay for living on the mountain. You can't get rich grooming dogs, but you can make decent money if you know your trade and are willing to work hard. I knew grooming, and I didn't drive down and up the mountain five days a week not to work hard. Every week I put money in my savings account to get ready to buy the place on the mountain that wasn't for sale.

In addition to grooming, I taught obedience training classes on Tuesday nights after I finished work at the shop. I was part of the City of Falls Church Parks and Recreation program. So was Bones. She had to come down with me on the days I had obedience training and wait around all day until we did our training at night. But she was a lady and never complained. Our classes—two each night—were made up of from fifteen to twenty people with all kinds of dogs. We trained in the basic exercises: heeling on a leash, sitting at heel on command, the long sit, the long down, coming on command. Bones really did the work, and I think she loved to show how good she was.

I like training. I think it is an important part of a good relationship between a person and a dog. In those days it was also a good way for me to put some extra money in my bank account.

I became friends with the woman who owned the house I was renting, and she finally agreed to sell it and, of course, the ten acres that went with it. It took me several years of grooming and obedience training to save enough money for the down payment. Those were years of not buying anything I didn't absolutely have to have; I would think a long time before buying a shirt or a pair of shoes. Jennifer and Kumar came up some weekends (for me that was Sunday and Monday), and she and I would occasionally go to a movie in Front Royal. That was the extent of my recreation during those years, the only money I spent "foolishly." But finally I had the money for the down payment, and I was able to work out a financing arrangement with the owner for the rest. At last the house and property were mine.

Slowly, doing all the work I could myself at night and on my days off, I converted the big utility workroom into a grooming room, built kennels and runs, and converted the garage into an indoor kennel-run area. I started my grooming business on the mountain a little at a time. When I had enough steady customers to fill up a day of grooming, I would drop a day from my Vienna schedule. Fortunately, grooming is the kind of work where such an arrangement is possible. As I worked less in Vienna, the owner of that shop gave more

21

Putting the finishing touches on a new kennel.

(Left) Building a new kennel for one of the runs. When Peggy works outside, Dare is her constant companion.

work to the other groomers she had and brought in another groomer part time.

Very few people wanted to drive up the mountain to deliver their dogs for grooming. What I did was buy an old Cherokee Jeep (later a Toyota pickup) and fill it with kennels. In the morning I would drive to Front Royal and other places and pick up dogs to be groomed. At the end of the day I would deliver their beautiful dogs back to the owners. It made a long day but not much longer than driving back and forth to Vienna.

Any kind of work has its good and bad features, I'm sure, and so does grooming: bad features, when a dog you thought was nice bites you or when you get a dog so matted from neglect that you break a blade trying to get it into his fur. But on the whole I like grooming. There's lots of variety: poodles, cockers, Lhasas, collies, Scotties—on and on. It's fun getting to know a dog over time, learning its personality. (Of course, there are always those you wish you didn't have to know.) I like making a dog look better and feel better, and they do feel better when they have been properly bathed and groomed. To take a dog that has had truly bad care, get rid of fleas, make it look like its breed is supposed to look—and try to educate the owner about proper care—gives me real satisfaction.

However, even before I was finished building up my new place, I did something else: I bought a puppy. I had been corresponding with kennel owners for over a year to find just the right female to start my breeding program. There was one kennel in New Jersey, Connie and Ted Beckhardt's Cobert Kennel, that I had heard about and read about and had great respect for. The Beckhardts have produced many champion German shepherds, including the great American and Canadian champion, Cobert's Reno. I wrote to Connie Beckhardt, told her my story and why I wanted to raise German shepherds, and asked her to help me find a good puppy to start with.

Connie was very helpful. She didn't have a female puppy at that time, but she put me in touch with Vito Moreno, owner of VeeMor Kennel. Connie said she had seen a puppy in a litter there that she thought had good potential. I called Mr. Moreno and made an appointment to drive to New Jersey and see the puppy. Jennifer went with me, and we took her car—she had a bigger one then—so that Kumar and Bones could go. Poor Doran had died of cancer—probably caused by his leg injury—the year before, so now I had only Bones.

The puppy I went to see was Dare, and she was beautiful. Mr. Moreno had bought Dare's mother from the Beckhardts. Her name was Cobert's Drama. Dare's father was Alborado of Rockledge, another good kennel. The price for Dare was five hundred dollars, reasonable for a puppy with show potential and such a fine pedigree, but a lot of money for me, especially at that time. But a foundation female like Dare was part of my plan, and I bought her.

I can't imagine what the ride back was like for Dare, with a big German shepherd that certainly was not her mother and a strange, long-haired male the likes of which she had never seen before. Dare was four months old and already twice Kumar's size, but this was his car, and he was clearly the boss. Even when she grew to be several times Kumar's size, Dare always treated him with great deference.

The trip back to my mountain in Virginia was a happy one for me. Now the pieces were complete. Now I could finish getting my place ready while I was waiting for Dare to grow up and give me beautiful puppies.

Three

Zoe

BUILDING this place has been fun. It is still fun, and that's a good thing because it is hard work, too, and lots and lots of hard work is still ahead. There have been problems, disappointments, unexpected twists and turns, and many, many happy days. But let me tell you about my worst day on the mountain because everything has seemed easier once I got through it.

First, I should say that when Dare was two years old I bred her to a German shepherd with a good pedigree and a good stud record. After four weeks, I took her to a vet in Front Royal, and his examination and palpation indicated that she was pregnant. I put her on a good pregnancy diet, and she got big, just as she was supposed to. I expected a litter of five or six or more, but then one of those unexpected twists came along. On the night of her delivery, Dare produced one puppy, and that was all. She produced Zoe.

Zoe soon after her first litter.

A single-puppy litter is not all that rare; still, it was a disappointment. I would have been more disappointed if Zoe hadn't been such a fine little German shepherd. Since she was an "only" puppy, she received a great deal more attention than most puppies get. Not from Dare: German shepherd mothers cut the silver cord pretty early so that their puppies will learn to fend for themselves. But I carried Zoe around, talked to her, played with her, let her go places with me. A great deal of bonding went on in those first months. I imagined the fine litters of puppies she would give me some day.

Now about that terrible day. It started like many of my days do: one of my shoes was missing. I looked under the bed, but I knew it wouldn't be there. Dare was lying on the floor beside my bed, where she always sleeps at night, but she looked away, paying no attention to what I was doing.

"Dare," I said, "did you take my shoe?"

She turned her head toward me when I said her name and gave me her wide-eyed innocent look. After a few seconds of my staring at her, she turned away again and yawned, a sure sign that she was nervous.

I don't remember exactly when it started, but it has been going on a long time now. When Dare is out-of-sorts with me about something, she takes one of my shoes during the night and hides it outdoors. It is always the left shoe; I have no idea why. And I never know when she is going to be upset with me or exactly why. Sometimes, I'm sure it's because I won't let her go to town with me when she expected to go. Sometimes it's because I make her go in the kennel when that is the last thing she wants to do. There are other things, like my being too tired at night to play enough ball with her. She remembers and after I've gone to sleep, she takes her revenge. I could put my shoes where she couldn't get them, I suppose,

Coyote, like the other dogs, gets a bath twice a month. In the fall tick and flea season, the bath may be even more frequent.

but I never know when she has stored up some grievance. Besides, she would just take something else.

"All right, Dare," I said. "Let's find my shoe."

I put on my houseshoes and started out, Dare following reluctantly. Bones was lying in the living room and didn't bother to look up; she knew what was going on. Zoe was outside, already investigating some interesting scent in a corner of the yard, busy getting the day started. She was still my

Flea and tick powder is a regular part of the good health routine.

beautiful firstborn on the mountain, no longer a puppy but at five months very much a little girl.

Dare trotted to a far part of the yard, so I knew not to look there; she always goes where she *hasn't* hidden my shoe. Zoe saw us and came over, but when she got close to one of my flower beds, Dare rushed her and chased her away. That was a dead giveaway. I went to the flower bed and found my shoe where Dare had dropped it among some black-eyed Susans.

"That wasn't so good, Dare," I said, picking up my shoe. "You've done lots better than this."

Dare looked annoyed and followed me back into the house. Since this was Monday, my day off, I had nothing to do but drive to Front Royal for groceries and supplies; repair a leak in a kennel roof; repaint a wall of my grooming room; sharpen scissors and repair a clipper; plant beans and squash; give Bones, Dare, and Zoe their biweekly dips against fleas and ticks; and have a long tennis ball session with Dare so that she would not hide my shoe again that night. Zoe was learning about playing ball and joined in; Bones loved tennis ball, too, but she was up in years and sick with a stomach tumor, so she just watched.

I was taking care of two dogs, Jake, a beautiful blond Laborador, and Ellie, a beautiful black. At dusk that day I went out to transfer them from the outdoor kennels to the inside kennels next to the grooming room. I let my dogs stay out at night if they want to because I know I can trust them and that they can take care of themselves, but I bring in dogs I am taking care of unless I know them very well.

Zoe went with me to get Jake and Ellie. Zoe and Jake trotted happily to the house; Ellie and I followed. Suddenly, Zoe gave a heart-stopping scream—there is no way to describe the sound except as a scream—and scrambled to the front door. As I ran to her, I looked down at where she had been and saw a snake, a small copperhead, coiled and ready to strike again.

I herded Jake and Ellie away from the copperhead, quickly put them in the inside kennels, and rushed back to Zoe, checking on the way to see that the snake was gone. Zoe was still huddled at the front door, crying. When I brought Zoe in the house, Dare and Bones rushed her. I think she sounded to them as if she were dying, and perhaps instinct told them to put her out of her misery. I pushed Dare and Bones away, picked Zoe up, and went into my bedroom, slamming the door.

I reached for the phone beside my bed and called the vet

closest to me, the vet in Front Royal. After two tries and two busy signals, I dialed the emergency number of Dr. Jack Love, the vet in Middleburg, and got him immediately at his home. My words tumbled out as I tried to tell him what had happened, and I'm sure he could tell that I was in a panic—which I was. This was my first experience with snakebite; I didn't know what to expect, but I knew Zoe might die if she didn't get proper treatment.

Dr. Love calmed me and reassured me. He told me to put a tourniquet on Zoe's leg. He stayed on the line while I took one of my long socks and tried to make a tourniquet; but I had no experience, and very quickly he told me to take it off since I might not have it right. He said to bring Zoe to the clinic immediately; he would meet me there. He said to keep Zoe lying down in the car and if possible to keep the leg on which she had been bitten below her body.

I carried Zoe out of the house—she weighed only fifty pounds at that time—and put her in the back seat of my little Volkswagen, dangling her leg over the edge of the seat to keep it below her body. She was quiet now, her crying stopped, so I hoped she would stay that way. Usually I don't like to drive the mountain in the dark, but tonight I never gave it a thought. My mind was only on one thing, getting to Middleburg, and we made it in forty-five minutes, which is good time.

Dr. Love was set up and waiting for us when I carried Zoe into the clinic and put her on the table. It had now been a little over an hour since she had been bitten. In the bright clinic light I could see that, in that short time, the two fang punctures where the poison had been injected had now become an open wound the size of a silver dollar, exposing tissue, tendons, and bone. The wound gave off an acidlike odor, and I could almost see the poison spreading.

Dr. Love went quickly and efficiently to work. By now Zoe was going into shock, her eyes glazed, her breathing shallow. Dr. Love put her on fluids, gave her injections of powerful antibiotics, and started topical treatment of the wound. As the doctor took control, the effects of my long day and the stress began to hit me. I started to feel dizzy and I stepped outside to breathe the cool night air. I kept asking myself, is she going to die? Is she going to be crippled? I had told Dr. Love that the copperhead that had bitten Zoe was a small one, hoping that would make some difference. He said that could be worse because young copperheads haven't learned to control the amount of poison they inject and may actually release more than an older, larger snake.

Feeling a little better, I went back into the clinic. Dr. Love was still working with Zoe, and I asked him how she was doing. He said she was going to be all right. He said that without speedy treatment of snakebite, amputation is sometimes necessary and secondary infections can be serious but that none of those things should be a problem for Zoe because I had brought her to the clinic in time. The doctor said that he would take her home with him for the night and that I probably could take her home the next day.

I left Zoe with Dr. Love, knowing that she was in loving, capable hands and drove back up the mountain. Dare and Bones greeted me happily; they looked for Zoe and were puzzled by her absence. We all settled in for the night, but I was restless and couldn't sleep. Dr. Love had been reassuring about Zoe's recovery, but I couldn't help worrying that some permanent damage might have been done.

When I called Dr. Love the next morning, he said that Zoe had had a good night. He would have let her come home, but I decided to leave her an extra day and night because I had obedience training classes Tuesday night. When I picked her up on Wednesday, we were both very happy to see each other. She wagged her tail, even though she was in great pain. I was shocked to see that her leg was swollen to three times its normal size. Dr. Love told me that this swelling would last for several weeks, that she would have to be kept in the house and taken out only for short walks on a lead. I would also have to continue topical treatment of her wound along with oral antibiotics for several weeks.

Dare and Bones were glad to see Zoe when she limped into the house. They both inspected her injury with great interest, and then they went about their business. It seemed to me that they were more considerate of her than usual during her recuperation, which took three weeks. Zoe was very stoic about her pain. She never whimpered when I was treating her wound; she just watched me intently. All of my German shepherds have always been easy to treat. They seem to understand that you are helping them and that you are in charge, the pack leader, the top dog. They quietly and without complaint accept whatever you must do.

As Dr. Love had predicted, Zoe completely recovered with no impairment whatever. The only evidence of that bad day on the mountain is an inch-long black scar on Zoe's foot, but the memory is in my head forever.

Zoe is not afraid of snakes and neither am I, but we have learned to have a healthy respect for the damage they can do. I have come to recognize Zoe's special high-pitched bark that says, "Danger! Snake!" And she knows that her "alarm" bark will bring me in a hurry, armed with a hoe.

Four

A Note on Names

LET ME take a minute to say a few things about naming dogs. If you buy a purebred puppy from a kennel, it may already have a name. Some kennels name their litters and register them with the American Kennel Club before they sell them. You, the owner, can call the puppy anything you want to— that will be its "call" name—but if you ever enter it in an AKC dog show or other AKC event or register its puppies, you must use its AKC-registered name.

When I bought Dare, her litter was already registered, and she had a name: VeeMor's Endless Love. In the future, on all AKC papers, she would always have to be identified as VeeMor's Endless Love. To me she will always be Dare, but to the AKC she will always be VeeMor's Endless Love. The American Kennel Club was organized in 1874 to maintain and improve the standards of purebred dogs. The AKC recognizes

Dare's name came from a suggestion by Peggy's mother, while Peggy's sister named Zoe.

and registers 124 different breeds. Today the AKC's ancestry registry contains the names and pedigrees of over 30 million dogs!

In most cases the kennel or owner you buy a purebred puppy from will give you an AKC Dog Registration Application. This application must be signed by the seller and must list the breed, sex, and color of the dog, its date of birth, the registered names of its sire and dam, and the name of the breeder. You can then enter the name of your choice on the application form. If you want to register your dog with the AKC, you should not buy a puppy if the owner does not give you a completed AKC registration application or a signed bill of sale or written statement that contains all of the information listed above.

You may wonder about Dare's rather unusual registered name: Endless Love. Kennel owners who name their dogs usually use one of two methods. One method is to give names alphabetically by litter. The first litter will have names starting with A: Abigail, Adam, Alfred, Amber, Apollo. The other method is to name all of the puppies in a litter according to a subject or theme. Dare's litter was named for popular songs, in her case, "Endless Love." Another of the puppies in her litter was "Earth Angel."

No matter what kind of dog you have, purebred or mixed breed, there are a few things to remember in choosing a name. In the first place, your dog won't care a bit what you call it. It will learn to respond to any name. But you and your family are going to hear your dog's name just as often as you hear the names of other family members. So the name should be one that the family likes, and the whole family should take part in picking the name. Part of the fun of having a dog is finding a name that has some special meaning for its owner or owners or that fits the dog's looks or personality.

And keep these two points in mind:

Short names tend to be better than long names. You can say them clearly and crisply. Give your dog a long name if you want to, but call it by a part of the name. Marmaduke can be Duke. Penelope can be Penny.

Avoid a name that sounds like the name of someone in your family. If your brother's name is Billy, don't call your dog Tillie. Tillie will jump every time you call Billy. When he doesn't want to answer, Billy will say he thought you were calling Tillie.

It should be obvious that some of my dogs' names— Doran, Bones—have come from people who meant something special to me. In a certain way that is true of Dare's name. My mother never forgets that Irish blood flows in our family's veins. She called me one day and said, "Peggy, I have just heard the most beautiful Irish name: Meagan Adair. Why don't you change your name to Meagan Adair O'Callaghan?"

I said I thought it was a little late for that, but I told her I would name my next dog Meagan Adair. The puppy I bought in New Jersey was the next, but Meagan Adair didn't seem right and neither did just Meagan or just Adair. And then I shortened Adair to Dare. That seemed right and still does.

And my mother liked it.

Five

Mountain Full of Puppies

Zoe's first litter was only two puppies, and one of those was stillborn. I wasn't discouraged, but since Dare was having trouble getting pregnant again, I certainly wasn't off to a very fast start in my puppy-raising program. And then one early spring, Dare and Zoe both produced full litters, Dare five puppies in March, Zoe six a month later in April. That was a busy time in the whelping closet and a busy time for me!

A wonderful time, too, a big part of what my life on the mountain is all about. If you love dogs, the puppy weeks are a special delight; and if you love German shepherds, there is simply nothing in the world like puppy time.

I weigh each puppy at birth—they weigh about a pound and will grow to seventy-five or a hundred times that!—and keep a weekly weight chart to track their physical development. Some breeders identify puppies by tying ribbons of

The good mother. Zoe with puppy from her first litter.

different colors around their necks or by some similar method, but I don't do that. From the very beginning, I try to find ways of distinguishing them: one will have two light-colored toes on his left front foot, one will have a big light-colored splash on her chest. And very quickly, their actions become identifying characteristics: some are quiet, some more active, some like to roughhouse, some are leaders. I think this kind of identification helps me get to know the puppies better and gives me better guidance in getting the right puppy and the right buyer together. I keep a diary on each puppy, but most of the information is stored in my head.

I handle the puppies every day from the very day of their birth, pick them up, talk to them, hold them on my lap. This human contact is an essential part of their socialization, to get

The puppies are Zoe's, but Dare (left) is quite comfortable with them.

them ready for the people they will spend their lives with. After a week I let the other dogs in for a peek at the puppies. That spring there was only Zoe to look at Dare's puppies and Dare to look at Zoe's. (Bones had died during the winter.) The dogs are intensely curious about the puppies. The new mother is never very friendly and sometimes shows her teeth a little, but she will let them have a look.

For the first two weeks, the puppies are on their mother's milk entirely. At that point I start to feed them a little ground beef. I roll it up into tiny balls, warming the meat with my hands. I pick the puppies up and feed them one at a time. Some puppies love the meatballs from the first bite; others won't touch them, but after two or three times they learn to like them.

A rare hand-fed treat between meals. Peggy feeds her dogs twice a day, an all-natural, specially ordered dry food, with special changes for the seasons and the dogs' individual needs.

The meatballs are the puppies' first introduction to eating on their own. At about three weeks I begin to feed them a gruel made of cereal, evaporated milk, honey, and raw egg yolk. At four weeks I introduce them to commercial puppy food that I put through a blender, and at five to six weeks they go on the commercial puppy food without benefit of the blender. They are still nursing all this time but getting less and less milk as the weeks go by; by six weeks nursing is more a security blanket than anything else, wanting to stay close to their mother. After six weeks and sometimes before, they will be completely weaned.

I name a litter of puppies as soon as I have thought of a theme and names within the theme that seem to fit the puppies or that mean something to me. Jennifer helped me and, since we are movie buffs, we named Dare's litter for movie stars: Coyote (Peter Coyote), The Duke (John Wayne), Hank (Henry Fonda), Greta (Greta Garbo), and Preston (Robert Preston). We named Zoe's litter for flowers, which is how Freesia got her name.

The puppies are up on their feet and moving around by three weeks, and by four weeks they are allowed to run around the kitchen, which is a good way to continue their socialization and expand their horizon beyond the whelping closet. At six weeks I begin their vaccination—a multiple shot for distemper, kennel cough, and other canine viral diseases. They get this vaccine two more times at three- to four-week intervals.

Now they are ready to see the big world beyond the house. Their mother is out there with them and—if the weather is good—they love to stay outdoors in the sun and explore all the fascinating mysteries of the yard. After a while I let them spend the nights in an outside kennel. They really prefer it to sleeping in the house; it is cool and there is plenty of room. There is no danger because the mother or one of the big dogs

For a German shepherd puppy even a bug in the grass is fascinating.

In good weather, the puppies like to eat and sleep in the outside kennels.

Drinking with the big guy.

will be sleeping outside, too, not in the kennel with the puppies but close by. I do usually take one of the puppies in the
house for the night to keep up the socialization process and
to let their individual personalities develop.

I have so many great pictures in my mind: three or four
of the puppies tumbling down a hill into a bed of leaves,
chasing frogs at the edge of the pond, learning to swim. The
first thing they try to do is walk on the water with their big

Bushed. These puppies found a rawhide chew belonging to one of the big dogs, dragged it around the yard and gnawed on it until they needed a nap.

paws. And it is fun to watch Dare with them. She doesn't like conflict and will break up a puppy fight if it gets rough, even if the puppies aren't hers. And she will push a puppy back if she thinks he is somewhere he shouldn't be.

Probably the most fun of all is to watch their personalities develop. Freesia is a good example. I kept her because I could see lots of good German shepherd characteristics in her and thought she would fit into my breeding program. Also, my mother had come for an extended visit, and she became quite fond of Freesia.

By the time she was six weeks old, Freesia was a dominant

Zoe looking a bit doubtfully at one of Dare's puppies.

Freesia (jumping) and Dare having fun with Peggy.

puppy. She liked to be right in the middle of things with the whole group; she would challenge the male puppies and take them on, even the bigger and older ones in Dare's litter. She still likes to roughhouse and play King of the Mountain. She will get up on a big rock or a hill and bark at Dare, Zoe, and Coyote until they try to chase her off. She has great agility and jumping ability. Once she jumped on the roof of my mother's new car to play King of the Mountain. My mother saw her and chased her off, but she jumped up there several other times. That strained their relationship, but Mother still loves her.

And Freesia is the most curious of all the dogs. As a puppy she was always the first one to investigate something new. Sometimes that got her into trouble. I saw her following a toad around the yard one day, but by the time I got to her, she had picked it up. Toads secrete poison through their skin, enough to make a puppy sick, and Freesia did get sick very quickly. I put her in the pickup and rushed her to the vet, who took care of her. But Freesia's first ride in the truck was a miserable one. The other dogs love truck rides, but to this day Freesia will do anything she can to avoid getting in it.

Sometimes Freesia's agility and curiosity combine to get her in real trouble. There is an embankment in my yard that, at its highest point, comes close to one corner of the roof of my house. One day Freesia leaped from the embankment onto the roof. When I saw her, she was walking around on the slanted roof like a mountain goat. She went to the high side where, if she had slipped, she would have fallen twenty feet. I had to get up on the roof and coax her back to the low side and make her jump back onto the embankment.

Freesia would still like to be dominant, but with Dare and Zoe outranking her, she has to be satisfied to dominate Coy-

Freesia tracking. German shepherds are noted for their keen noses and tracking ability, which, together with their courage, have made the breed prized in police work.

ote. Fortunately, he is so relaxed, so laid back, I don't think he knows he is being dominated.

As a puppy, Coyote was aloof but friendly when approached, just the way a good German shepherd should be. He liked to spend time by himself; he wasn't timid or shy, just reserved. He is still the most reserved of the four dogs with outsiders. Coyote has a sharp intelligence; he was the first of the puppies to learn to swim, just by watching Zoe and his mother, Dare, and seeing how they did it. He has the best nose and is the best tracker. He is definitely the best at sensing an unknown presence in the area—man or beast.

Raising puppies isn't all fun. I look at Coyote today, and I see a big, handsome German shepherd. He has the confor-

Elbow problems do not keep Coyote from enjoying a run in the woods.

mation—the structure and angulation—the temperament and intelligence possibly to have been a good show dog, maybe a champion. I could have sold him for eight hundred dollars when he was three months old; I had an offer from a man who also saw the show potential in him.

But I thought I might want to keep him and show him and use him as a stud dog. And I'm glad I didn't sell him because by the time he was four months old, he was limping and in pain. I took him to the vet and the diagnosis was elbow dysplasia, an abnormal structural growth in the elbows of his front legs. In this genetic disease, the bones of the elbow joints don't mesh properly and then become fused in an abnormal way. The results are lameness and pain.

Research is showing that there is a genetic tendency for the problem to develop, with the actual cause being trauma—an injury to that area. The injury might even occur during rough puppy play and probably did in Coyote's case.

I had Coyote operated on when he was six months old. The operation was successful in that it cured his lameness and took away the pain. His gait is a little stiff now, his fluid running motion or "reach" not quite what it should be, but when he is out for a morning run with me or following a game trail, few people would see anything wrong. The operation cost five hundred dollars that I didn't really have, but every time I see Coyote running down a trail chasing something he sees or thinks he sees, I'm glad I found the money.

I could never use him to sire puppies, of course. The elbow dysplasia might never show up in his offspring, but it wouldn't be right to take that chance. I had Coyote altered, and he will live his life as a companion, a good friend who will make my life a little richer.

I WANT to say something about breeding. I breed for the standard, structurally correct, sound in mind and body German shepherd. My goal is to produce German shepherds capable of being show dogs—good enough to compete for championship or best dog titles in AKC competitions. A "show" dog is supposed to be the embodiment of everything a German shepherd should be: noble, sound in mind and body, capable of doing the work he was bred for, whether it be long hours of herding sheep, guiding the blind, doing police or military work as guard or tracker, showing his intelligence and agility in competing for obedience titles, or being a good companion.

Producing a champion takes some luck, combined with a

Coyote doesn't look entirely happy with the snow.

sound breeding program: a combination of structurally and
mentally correct dogs, long hours of studying pedigrees and
analyzing the dogs to be bred. I always hope to come up with
a show puppy or even a whole litter of show puppies because
there is no sense in breeding if you don't aim for perfection.

I realize that not every puppy will have show potential,
and I know that most will go to homes as pets and companions. But anyone who buys a German shepherd is entitled to
a good one.

Six

Letting Them Go

You PUT a lot of yourself into a puppy. When the time comes to sell it, you are beginning to feel that no one is good enough for it. That is foolish, of course. My main reason for being on this mountain is to produce good German shepherd puppies for people who really want them.

I do not sell puppies until they are at least eight weeks old. I know one or two experienced breeders who can evaluate their puppies well enough to sell them at seven weeks, but I am not one of those. I want to be as sure as I can be of a puppy's physical soundness and I want to know as much as possible about its personality before I introduce it to a prospective buyer.

By the same token, I try to find out as much as I can about a person or family that wants to consider buying one of my puppies. I want to know about where they live; German shep-

Cassie, one of Zoe's puppies.

herds should have a fenced yard or good-sized enclosed area. I like to know why they want a German shepherd. I am most reassured when they are replacing a dog—usually because of death—that they have had for a long time. I am doubtful if they have very young children, younger than seven or eight. I just say no if all they want is a guard dog. A German shepherd provides some security just by its presence, but to be a real guard dog requires highly skilled training or its temperament will be ruined. I am most happy when a potential buyer is

Zoe is starting to shed, "blowing coat," in the language of German shepherd raisers. "The mother always seems to be blowing coat when people come to see the puppies," Peggy says, "and she looks terrible."

referred to me by somebody I know. But most of my puppies are sold as a result of advertisements I place in the *Washington Post*, so I don't know the buyers until I talk with them.

Sometimes a doubtful situation works out if the people who want the dog are really committed. I remember one young couple who came to look at puppies; they had a girl of about four and a two-year-old son. That was not promising. But I didn't think the question of their buying a puppy would even come up after what happened. The little girl was throwing rocks and wouldn't stop when told to. Dare was present because her puppies were being shown. After a while she simply lost patience with the little girl; she walked over and pulled her by the shirt—not roughly but persistently—until she stopped.

A little later the two-year old was making a great fuss with lots of noise and paid no attention to his parents' efforts to quiet him. When Dare had had enough, she picked him up by his diaper, just as she might pick up one of her puppies, and set him down on the ground. The little boy stopped howling.

Well, I thought, there'll be no German shepherd puppy sold this morning.

And there wasn't. But the couple came back a few days later to look again. A second drive of thirty miles or so from their home and a second trip up the mountain was some evidence that their interest was real. They had both grown up with dogs, and they wanted a dog now for themselves and not for their children to play with. They chose a mild-mannered, sweet-tempered female. I still had my doubts, but this was a purchase I was able to keep in touch with, and I'm happy to say it has worked out.

Most of all, I try to assure myself that the buyer is prepared to make a commitment for the life of the dog, a commitment to its welfare. There is no way to know that will happen, but I try.

Seven

Training

F OR ME the greatest pleasure in having a dog is the interaction and communication between us, and both interaction and communication depend primarily on training. The more a dog learns, the more his horizons will be expanded, the more responsive and interesting he will be as a companion for you. The more you teach your dog, the more a team you are— and you are the team leader. Being responsive to commands can also be very beneficial to a dog. There may be times when obeying your command to heel, sit, or stay in place will keep him out of trouble or even save his life—or yours!

What I have just said applies to any breed of dog, any purebred, any mixed breed. Since I am an owner of German shepherds, I can say this with certainty to anyone who buys a German shepherd puppy: until you work with him in obedience training, you won't fully understand his remarkable intelligence, and you won't develop the character that is inherent in his breed.

Puppies learn from the day they are born and training should begin from the day you get your puppy. I am talking about "puppy" training, not formal training. It is important for your rapport with your puppy for him to be housebroken as soon as possible, to be taught not to chew on shoes and furniture, not to jump up on people, and to learn other simple rules of good conduct.

Whenever I sell a puppy, I give the new owner the puppy's health record and instructions on health care, feeding, and training. There are some good books on dog training, and I recommend that a new puppy owner get one of them. Two that I know are particularly good are *Expert Obedience Training for Dogs* by Winifred G. Strickland and *Mother Knows Best: The Natural Way to Train Your Dog* by Carol Lea Benjamin. These books cover everything from puppy training through advanced obedience training. I also tell buyers about obedience training courses near where they live if I know about them.

I think every dog owner should go through at least one obedience training course with his dog. Older dogs can do well in obedience courses, but naturally it is better to start young. Some programs have a "puppy kindergarten" for puppies from three to six months old. The classes are shorter, and there is a little more playtime. If puppy kindergarten is not available, your puppy from four months on should do fine in a regular novice or beginning obedience class.

Like all schools and all education, some obedience courses are better than others, and the determining factor almost always is the skill, experience, and patience of the instructor. In a good obedience course you will learn right along with your dog. The fact is that what you learn is the most important part of obedience training because it will enable you to train your dog in the obedience exercises he is learning in the course. Your home practice is the only way he will become truly responsive to the commands.

Even if you feel that you know enough to train your dog by yourself, with or without the help of a book, putting him through an obedience class is still a good idea. He will learn how to listen to you and not be distracted when there are other dogs around. Practicing in a group will improve his concentration and yours, too. And you will learn from seeing the mistakes and progress of your classmates and their dogs. Seeing that everyone has problems will help with any discouragement you might be feeling.

I have found in my obedience courses that children from age eight on can make great trainers. They have a natural companion relationship with their dog; they often have more patience; and when their dog learns a command, they feel genuine delight in what the two of them have accomplished together. Teenagers can be wonderful in training, too, if they are not into so many things that they can't give the obedience training the time and attention it has to have.

A good obedience course will help you train your dog to heel on a leash, heel without a leash, stand for examination, sit or lie down when you tell him to, hold that position even if you are out of sight, and come to you when you call him. These are the basic or novice exercises covered in American Kennel Club obedience trials for awarding the title of Companion Dog (C.D.).

Obedience training that you do with your dog on your own takes time and patience. I try to give a minimum of one-half hour a day five days a week to each dog in the basic obedience commands. I have found that a good time for obedience work is late afternoon or early evening before I feed them. Dogs get bored quickly, so I don't always start with

Ball, anyone?

the same commands, such as heel or stay, and I change the order and add new commands to the routine. When I am working with more than one dog, I switch the commands around and give each dog a turn. And after training I try to take the time to do something they will enjoy, like taking a walk or playing ball. Your dog will have a lot more patience if he knows that some fun is coming after the work.

In a sense, training goes on all the time. For example, if my dogs start misbehaving in the house, barking at each other or fighting, I will put them on a sit-stay and make them give me the all-important eye contact before they can move, even to go outdoors. That always calms them down.

Peggy is proud, but Zoe seems nonchalant about winning her Companion Dog title.

And when I talk to them throughout the day, I very carefully repeat the same phrases:

Go find the ball.

Do you want to ride in the truck?

Let's take a break.

Go to the pen.

Time for bed.

Let's play ball.

Do you want to eat?

No more.

Go find Peggy (a phrase used by my mother).

I have calculated that my dogs know probably a hundred key words or phrases that they have learned through my constant repetition.

The AKC certificate for Companion Dog is not easy to win. Your dog competes for points with other dogs and must be judged successful in the obedience exercise by three different judges at three different obedience trials. Bones earned her C.D. certificate, and Zoe has earned hers. I intend for Zoe to get her Companion Dog Excellent (C.D.X.) certificate. The C.D.X. title requires passing seven exercises—after the dog has attained his C.D. title—such as retrieving in a flat area as well as over a high jump and making a successful broad jump. Freesia is getting ready to enter AKC obedience trials, and I am sure that with her intelligence and agility, I will be able to put both C.D. and C.D.X. after her name in a year or two.

Dare does not have her C.D. certificate, and that is my fault. When she was young and vigorous, I was just too busy and didn't have the time to take her around to AKC obedience trials. Of course, Dare doesn't care a bit that she doesn't have C.D. behind her name. She knows how good she is. She loves to show off as my helper when I teach obedience classes.

But in my mind I know that Dare deserves her C.D. title, and I think we may still go through the AKC obedience trials together. Dare will probably think the other dogs around her are a bunch of beginners and will have a lot of fun teaching them.

Eight

Having Fun

Having a dog as a companion means enjoying each other's company, having fun together. Having four means having lots of fun! Five days a week I take an early-morning run with Dare, Zoe, Freesia, and Coyote. I run three miles on the road, and each day I alternate each dog on a lead so that he or she runs part of the distance with me. Just like a person, a dog needs to be conditioned slowly to this kind of exercise. You cannot take an unconditioned dog out for a three-mile run without risk of injury.

The three dogs not on a lead will keep up with me for a short time but then strike off into the woods to explore game trails or chase squirrels. They know where I am and are always back with me at the end of the run. Sometimes we are joined on our run by an owl that flies along with us. I can't imagine why he does this, but he has made himself a part of our early-

On the old wagon road in back of Peggy's place.

Summer fun at the pond on Peggy's place.

morning exercise for a long time now. The owl also hoots at night, and after a while that will give Coyote an excuse to start howling, which he loves to do.

There is a mud pond near the road made by a seeping spring. On really hot days the dogs like to stop at that spot and wallow in the cool mud. They are incredibly dirty when they come out, and we always go to the pond below our house where they have a swim and get clean before we go home.

At times I take just one or two of the dogs and go for a

Zoe having fun at the park but also learning to jump on command.

walk on one of the trails in the woods. Occasionally we meet a lost hiker and help him find his way back to the Appalachian Trail. On one walk I had Dare on a lead and was letting Coyote run free. He disappeared into the woods, and a few minutes later a deer came flying down the path toward Dare and me. I'm sure Coyote must have been trailing the deer and frightened it. The deer came to a stop about thirty feet from us. Dare, of course, was dancing around and barking, but the deer seemed to sense that the dog could not get to her and that I was not a threat. She just stood there for what seemed

The dogs are interested in the work Peggy is doing, but Dare drops a tennis ball to try to entice her into a little playtime.

like minutes, staring at us and testing the air with her nose. Then I heard the brush rustling and so did the deer. He trotted back into the woods just as Coyote appeared, excited by the chase. He ran over to us, and we walked on together.

I try to do something with the dogs each day after work: a long game of tennis ball, a nice walk in the evening, a session at the pond retrieving sticks thrown in the water. Sometimes I am just too tired for the after-work activity, but when I skip it, I usually pay a price. The dogs probably will get into some mischief in the house or let their wrestling and roughhousing

Freesia with Peggy climbing the agility ladder.

Freesia and Zoe learning to jump on command.

get out of control. They may even break through the fence; that has happened more than once.

Occasionally on Sunday or Monday I will take two of the dogs to the park in Front Royal but never more than two at a time. Usually I take Zoe and Freesia because they are in training for AKC obedience titles and need to be worked out in many different situations. They jump, climb on the jungle gym, and even slide down the slide. Children in the park gather around to watch and cheer. Zoe and Freesia love showing off and will keep going as long as I let them.

Sometimes companionship is just sitting around quietly together on the porch, enjoying a lovely late spring or early fall evening on the mountain.

Nine

Zoe Saves
the Day

Zoe was named by my sister; at least she suggested the name. She knew I was disappointed that Dare's first litter was a single puppy. She called me and said, "Why don't you name her Zoe?" She told me Zoe was a Greek name, a feminine name that means life; and the little puppy was life, life from Dare. And so she became Zoe.

I don't think owners with more than one dog should have a favorite—just like parents shouldn't have a favorite child. So Zoe isn't my favorite; let's just say she is very special. She was, after all, my first puppy born on the mountain; and, as I have said, since she was a one-puppy litter, I gave her a lot of extra attention, and there was more bonding between us than with the later dogs. And, of course, I nursed her through her copperhead poisoning.

There's no question that Zoe is possessive of me, but she's

Zoe training for her Companion Dog Excellent title. She must learn to retrieve the dumbbell over a high jump and in a flat area. Here she is just beginning to learn the preliminary "get it" and "hold it" commands.

not a clinger. She likes to be with the other dogs and gets along with them well. She is easygoing and accepts new people more quickly than Dare, Freesia, and Coyote. All in all, I guess you would say that Zoe is the dog everyone would like to take home.

Not that she's perfect. In obedience work she has excellent "dog" attention for the next command, better than any of the others. That is because she always looks at you; she has unusually good eye contact. And yet the first two times I took her to obedience trials she did goofy things that really embarrassed me. I had been bragging about her great eye contact, and then in the recall exercise, she just wouldn't look at me! I was mortified. Zoe is possessive of her leash when she is in strange places because to her it means going home. Once, one of the ring stewards was holding her leash, and she trotted over to him, which is just what she shouldn't have done. Another time when I told her to stay in place, I discovered that she was walking along quietly behind me.

At home Zoe is the game player of the four dogs, the instigator of a lot of the mischief they get into. She tries to get everyone going. She will "see" some imaginary thing in a far part of the yard and go charging toward it with the other three dogs at her heels, barking at the top of their voices. Or she will start them digging in a place where they shouldn't dig and then wander off, leaving them to get the blame.

Those are just little things that prove she's not perfect, and she is still very special.

One evening in May after she had her puppies, Zoe showed her true colors and proved—more than any dog show medal or obedience trial ribbon could—what a fine German shepherd she is. It was dusk, and I had just put the pups up in an outside kennel. As I came back into the house, Zoe, who had stayed outside, started barking. It took me a few seconds to realize that this was no ordinary bark but her "alarm" bark, which means only one thing: danger at hand.

I ran out and saw Zoe following a three-foot-long copperhead that was slithering toward a rock pile near the back corner of the house. Zoe was maintaining a careful one-to-two-foot distance behind the snake and continuing her alarm bark. Just at that moment, the copperhead disappeared into the rock pile, a stack of large stones left over from the building of a retaining wall over a year ago. I just hadn't got around to getting rid of them.

I ran back to the house and called to my mother to keep Dare inside. I grabbed a hoe, a flashlight, and the big plastic jug of Clorox, which I had been told was good for flushing a snake out of a hiding place. No time for panic now, I told myself grimly, just kill the copperhead. I commanded Zoe to stand back, and she obeyed, moving just a few feet away from the rock pile. She knew the snake was in there, but I was in charge now, and she was content just to keep up her barking.

I aimed the flashlight at the rocks and poured Clorox in several places. Immediately the snake popped its head out of the rocks. Now I was in a dilemma. I had the flashlight in one hand, the Clorox in the other, the hoe under my arm. I needed another hand! I had to pour more Clorox to drive the snake out, but I had to have a free hand to try to chop him with the hoe—and two hands on the hoe would be better!

I decided to set the flashlight on the ground, trying to keep it trained on the rock pile and the snake. As I carefully lowered the flashlight, Zoe suddenly rushed toward me, snarling ferociously. I looked down and there, only a few inches from my hand, was another copperhead, coiled and ready to strike.

I jumped back, dropping the Clorox and shifting the hoe to my free hand. I brought the hoe down on the snake, severing its head. It was a lucky hit just when I needed some

Peggy insisting on eye contact from all her dogs.

Zoe, Freesia, and Dare pay close attention to Peggy. Coyote sees something else that needs watching.

luck. Not much of the Clorox had spilled. I picked up the jug and poured some more over the rocks, then dropped it again and got ready with flashlight and hoe. Three more copperheads slithered out of the rocks, and I quickly killed them.

Zoe kept up her barking, but at my command, she held her place. The whole thing was over in two minutes or less. My heart was pounding, my stomach was churning, but the copperheads were dead, and I was all right—thanks to Zoe.

I had to gather up the dead snakes and throw them away, an unpleasant task if there ever was one. Zoe watched me intently, but she had stopped barking.

Zoe's reward was a big hug and praise for her courage and a job well done. I'm sure that was all the reward she expected or wanted.

I HAVE been here in the Blue Ridge for almost ten years now. Some of my friends think I have the greatest life in the world. Some of them think I'm crazy. Maybe all of them are right. There are times when the work here is almost too much; by the end of the week on Saturday night sometimes I'm so tired I can hardly move. And there is always a new problem to solve. But I do have a great life here on the mountain, a life I love. And I *am* crazy—crazy about German shepherds.

Freesia with her first litter, four females and three males. Peggy and Jennifer had been handling the puppies, and Freesia seems to be counting them to make sure they are all back in place. For the first time—because of their number and similarity of markings—Peggy has had to use colored ribbons to help her identify the puppies.

Ten

A Letter from Peggy

JUST as *Crazy About German Shepherds* was going to press, I received this word from Peggy about Freesia's first litter:

"I wish you could come up here to see the 'Magnificent Seven.' They are a very special group and are being spoiled by all their relatives. Great-grandma Dare watches over them but keeps her distance. She is ever alert to any cries of distress and quickly responds by getting me to go with her to check the puppies.

"Zoe is the doting grandma and takes care of them as if they were her own, even lying down to nurse them (although she has no milk). Coyote has become Uncle Pete, and a loving uncle he is, now that they are over four weeks old and allowed to play outside. He plays with them, licks and cleans them, and shows great agility in never once stepping on them or hurting them. They are not afraid of him and bark at him and pull on his legs, neck, and tail.

"Freesia is, of course, the proud mama and an excellent one, too, though she is beginning to look a little frazzled."

Bibliography

Ainsworth, Ivy. "Then and now: German Shepherd Dogs Full Circle." *Purebred Dogs/American Kennel Gazette*, March, 1988.

"A Talk with Connie and Ted Beckhardt." *The German Shepherd Quarterly*, Winter, 1982/83.

Benjamin, Carol Lea. *Mother Knows Best: The Natural Way to Train Your Dog*. New York: Howell Book House, Inc., 1985.

The Complete Dog Book: Official Publication of the American Kennel Club. New York: Howell Book House, Inc., 1988.

The Monks of New Skete. *How to Be Your Dog's Best Friend: A Training Manual for Dog Owners*. Boston: Little, Brown and Company, 1979.

Mueller, Betty A. "Where Did You Get That Dog?" *German Shepherd Dog Review*, October, 1989.

Strickland, Winifred G. *Expert Obedience Training for Dogs*. New York: Macmillan Publishing Company, 1976.

—— and James Anthony Moses. *The German Shepherd Today*. New York: Macmillan Publishing Company, 1974.

Index

American Kennel Club
   (AKC), 35, 38, 53, 64, 65
Appalachian Trail, 20, 69

Beckhardt, Connie, 24–25
Beckhardt, Ted, 24
Blue Ridge Mountains, 3

Charlottesville, VA, 11
Cobert Kennel, 24
Companion Dog, C.D. (AKC
   title), 64
Companion Dog Excellent,
   C.D.X. (AKC title), 64

Dog grooming, 20, 21, 24

Dog names
   advice about naming, 38–39
   AKC registration of, 38
   kennel and call names, 35,
      44

Elbow dysplasia (genetic canine disease), 52–53

Front Royal, VA, 9, 17, 31,
   72

German shepherds
   breeding, 53–54
   characteristics of, 51, 53

Love, Dr. Jack, 32–34

Manassas, VA, 12–13
Middleburg, VA, 17
Moreno, Vito, 25

Puppies
    care of, 40–42, 44, 46
    selling, 55–58
    training, 60

Shenandoah National Park, 17
Snakebite, 31–34

Training
    home practice, 60–62, 64
    importance of, 59–60
    obedience classes, 60–61
    puppy, 60

VeeMor Kennel, 25
Vienna, VA, 20